The Faithful Five and The Purple Forest

Chris Aldridge

Cover illustrated by Toby Aldridge

A catalog record for this book is available from the National Library of New Zealand.

ISBN: 978-0-473-59550-0

I dedicate this book to all those who have helped bring out the best in others. People like you make life beautiful.

CONTENTS

ACKNOWLEDGMENTS

Thank you to everyone who read my draft copy of this book and encouraged me that it was worth sharing with others. As promised, I will let you know when I have finished the next book.
Thank you to Toby for drawing the cover picture at short notice.
Thank you to Brigitte who helped me to publish this book.
Thank you to my family and my spiritual brothers.
Thank you to those above who guided me with writing this story. I couldn't have done this without you.
None of our accomplishments in life are in isolation. For every step of our journey there has been help in one form or another. We are meant to be there for each other in this life.

GINGER

Her name was Ginger. Not her real name of course, but the one we gave her. She was magical, light in her movements, and a face like a porcelain doll. Although she looked like a beautiful angel, none of us were jealous of her. Ginger had a way about her that made you want to be with her. They say that light attracts light and like flowers open up to greet the sun we were the same when Ginger was around. Certainly, for us when Ginger was around our worlds lit up big time. Not that we were sad or angry, but Ginge (what we sometimes called her as short for Ginger) brought out a feeling of happiness in us each time we were with her.

I think we were five when we first met. Our little friendship gang started off with the two of us and then we became The Faithful Five with Ted, Michael and Joss. Together we were quite a strange bunch. Not strange as in weird clothing or rainbow coloured hair. We all came from different family backgrounds and I'm not sure we would have been friends had it not been for Ginger. In the beginning we were all her friends and in doing so we became friends with each other. And as our childhood years went by our bonds of friendship strengthened with each passing year.

We stuck together as a group even after Ginger moved away. Yes, she moved away in our teenage years. But, before Ginger left, when we were 12 we had the first of many amazing and incredible experiences with her. Somehow, we could see the world differently… Really, I'm not joking, it's like we travelled to a different world. It was during those experiences that we promised to stick together as friends and never ever give up on each other.

Our first experience was when we travelled via our minds at the end of our summer break. Hang on, before you ask too many questions, I'm about to explain. We had been down to our local and favourite river many times before but this time when we went down it was different. We thought we were just going down to swim and play tag and eat our picnic lunches that we had made, the usual fun stuff, but not this time. We didn't know our perception of our world was about to change, for the better.

This time at the river everything seemed different. Ginger's hair seemed to really shine the closer we got to the river. And the river seemed to sparkle more the closer we got to it, like the river was full of diamonds. We all seemed to notice her hair and the river, and we became quite mesmerised watching the two. Joss, who was a brunette, started looking at her hair to see if it was shining the same. Michael and Ted tried to give her a look with their eyes to say her hair was shining the same, but truth be told, it wasn't.

Ginger spoke in her usual soft voice, "I have a treat planned for us today but before we start you must all promise me and each other that you won't tell another soul. It is important that until we agree as a group that what we are about to do is not spoken about to anyone. Will you all promise me and each other that this will remain our secret?"

I felt that Ginger already knew that we would keep this to ourselves, or she wouldn't have even mentioned it to us. So, we stood in a circle and each one of us put our right hand on our heart and our left hand on top of each other's hands. We then promised Ginger and each other that with full respect to ourselves and each other we would not share this with another soul. We looked each other in the eyes as we said this. Ginger then explained why we had made the promise. She said that there were people out there that would exploit her gifts. Ginger called them gifts instead of talents because she felt she had been given some amazing powers that she called presents from the universe. She winked with a cheeky grin when she said that the presents were gift wrapped in her beautiful body. As we were almost teenagers at the time, we didn't quite understand why she would want to keep such a secret. People would go to movies to watch fantasies about people with magical powers and here we had a friend that actually had them. How cool was that! She could be rich and famous like some kids dream of being.... but later as we saw what she could do, we understood why we had to keep such a secret.

At Ginger's request we then sat in a circle and held hands. We hadn't held hands before as that was something that lovers did, so we giggled for a bit out of shyness before we went silent. For some strange reason we all got a clear understanding that to tell anyone about Ginger's talents would be detrimental to Ginger. We looked into each other's eyes and nodded. It was as if we could read or hear each other's thoughts whispering to each other. Ginger was very precious to us and the last thing any of us wanted was for something bad to happen to her, well to any of us actually.

We sat close to the river, and I could hear the sound of the water as it would stop and alter its direction around the odd rock. There was a gentle breeze that day which helped keep the summer day from being a really hot sizzler. The trees looked like they were enjoying the breeze as the tops seemed to be dancing each time a puff of air went by. Ginger looked at each of us. First Michael, then me, then Joss then Ted. We looked back at her and then to each other. I knew Ginger was about to blow our minds although I never would have guessed how in a million years.

Ginger closed her eyes and took a deep breath and then slowly let it out. Then she kept breathing like this and then there wasn't a sound to be heard other than the river and her deep breathing. We started to do the same, we took a deep breath in through our noses and filled our bellies with air and then slowly let the air out through our mouths. Then we kept breathing like this. The thoughts in my head disappeared as we concentrated on our breath. Then an awareness popped into my head, I couldn't hear the river anymore. I tried to listen for the sound of water but I couldn't hear it. Just as I realised this Ginger softly said, "Open your eyes guys." And so we did.

Ginger had taken us away somehow. We were still holding hands but everything around us had changed. I started to get scared and noticed all of us looked quite anxious actually. We then looked at Ginger and she looked excited, and I guess it was the excited look on her face that stopped us worrying. We then felt safe, and you could tell as all of our shoulders seemed to drop away from our ears to where they should be.

We were in what looked to be a meadow or forest but instead of green fields, they were purple and same with all the trees. Even the leaves and branches were purple although different shades. I never realised how many shades of purple existed… dark, light, dull and bright, some with pink tinges and some with blue. The place seemed magical and with such incredible dazzling beauty. I thought to myself, well this is grand!

We sat there looking around and staring for ages and then it seemed like Joss wanted to say something, but all Ginger did was look at her and mouth the word shhh.

No sooner had I looked at Joss and then at Ginger then I could hear the river again. I realised the reason I could hear the river again was because we were sitting back beside it. We were back in the land of green grass and blue sparkling rivers. Although the river didn't seem to sparkle as much as it had before when we had held hands. Ginger looked at us whilst we were checking out our familiar home surroundings and then she spoke. "So, what did you guys think?"

I asked if we could go back as I assumed we had all seen the same thing. Then simultaneously we asked, "Where were we?" Then we all started talking over each other in excitement saying things like, it seemed really peaceful… the colour purple, what was that about? Is there more...?

Ginger reminded us that we needed to get home. The sky was getting dark, and our parents would start to worry about us. I didn't realise how long we had been away; we hadn't even eaten our lunch. The travel only seemed like a few minutes but in reality, the whole experience had taken hours out of our day. Ginger promised to tell us about our adventure when we next met in the daytime. She said that our first time was the hardest and therefore took longer to get there but travel would get easier on each visit. We agreed to meet on Saturday, almost a week away. It's amazing when you really want something that time seems to go so slowly. Why is that?

THAT NIGHT

We all went home excited about what we had seen. I got home in time to set the table for dinner. I had fed my lunch to the birds on the way home so I would be hungry for dinner and by then I was actually starving. I never told mum when I fed the birds as she didn't like food being wasted.

"What's for dinner?" I asked mum.

"I'm trying a new recipe from Rachel" mum said.

"Who, Ginger's mum?" I asked.

"Yes, I popped over to say hi to her and talk about the school fair next month. Rachel said that she had a few things to do for it and then she gave me a recipe to try. I didn't think I would make it tonight as I wasn't sure I would have all the ingredients, but it turns out I had all of them. As you know they don't eat meat, actually they don't eat any animal products, so I guess her recipes involve lots of spices and herbs to make them tasty".

"That's great mum. I always feel full but light after eating those kinds of meals" I said. The truth was I preferred Rachel's meals to mums, but I didn't want to say anything as I love my mum big time.

"I also suggested to Rachel that we go and join you all at the river, but she said we should leave you guys to enjoy your time together given that the holidays are almost over."

Well, that would have been grand you think. Here we were all doing OUR thing and imagine my Mum popping in just as we were leaving or arriving back from the purple forest.

"Yeah, good idea of Rachel's to leave us to it" I said not really knowing what to say to my mum. So, I figured the less I said the better. I'm sure you will agree.

As we were eating our dinner that night all I could think of was the purple forest, the purple grass and… well…. everything that was shades of purple. I wanted to stay longer. I wanted to see Ginger now. I wanted to go back and explore. But it was dark and soon it would be my bedtime. I didn't want the day to end although it was almost over.

I did all my usual chores after dinner including brushing and flossing my teeth and putting my clothes away. I quickly kissed mum and dad goodnight and then went to my room and changed into my P.J.s. I jumped into bed looking forward to tomorrow. I just lay there thinking of the day and what I had seen. To me sleep seemed boring. Why waste time in bed when we could be in a purple wonderland. What else was there to see? I really wanted to tell mum about it at dinner, but I knew she wouldn't understand, let alone that this was a secret to be kept. I knew she was friends with Ginger's mum Rachel, and I had no idea what they talked about or got up to. I assumed nothing except drinking hot cups of tea and well, sharing recipes.

All of a sudden, my eyes just wanted to shut. As I was trying to resist, I went from seeing bits of my room from the moonlight in the gaps of my bedroom curtains to purple meadows when my eyes closed.

I couldn't believe it, every time my eyes closed, I saw purple. So, I decided not to resist sleep, especially if dreaming was going to remind me of the purple fields and trees. Imagine that.... sooo exciting.

It didn't take me long to fall asleep at all. But I'm not sure I was really asleep as I was back in the land of purple. I smiled to myself and wondered if the others were dreaming about the day as well. I thought I heard noises, so I turned towards the sounds. There was nothing scary about this place as it was really peaceful and so I wasn't scared when I heard the voices. All of a sudden Michael and Ted were walking towards me.

"Hi" I said in a high-pitched voice as I was surprised to see them in my dream. "Are we all in the same dream? Did you fall asleep?"

"Far out man!" Michael said in an excited and nervous voice, then doubting himself Michael asked, "Did you fall asleep?"

"Yep, so that means Joss and Ginger might be here soon" I replied.

I knew that both Joss and Ginger went to bed later than the rest of us. We joked that they were night owls whilst we were morning larks. I used to envy how they were allowed to go to bed later than me but then I loved getting up early in the morning as going to bed early meant I was up with the sun. Vampires don't like the sun, so I know I'm not one. That was me trying to make a joke by the way.

"Hi guys" said Joss. I was pleased to see her. Joss then asked "Did you guys know we would end up back here when we fell asleep"

"Nope" we all exclaimed together.

I'm not even sure we knew if this was real or a dream. Sometimes dreams seem so real it is hard to know the difference. That feeling that when you do wake up you pinch yourself to see if you are really awake and in your own bed in your own room.

Joss said, “This is incredible in that we have gone to sleep and now we are back together again in the purple forest.”

We just stood there nodding in agreement. What else was there to add?

This was incredible… well unbelievable actually. But I swear this is how it happened. Ginger had changed our lives and would continue for the next few years, this time around anyway.

It was strange in that we were all asleep and yet supposedly wide awake. We went to bed alone in our own beds and now here we were all standing and talking together just like any other day. But this wasn’t the day, this was supposed to be night and we were supposed to be in our own dream lands.

All of a sudden Joss disappeared. We started to panic, and all started to look around for her. How could Joss be here one minute and then gone the next? Would we be next? Ginger then turned up and answered us as if she had read our minds. “Calm down, Joss will be back soon. Her dad has woken her and so she won’t be back with us until she falls back asleep.” We all stood there anxiously waiting for Joss, wondering how Ginger knew this although we believed her anyway.

“Hi guys, I’m back! Sorry about that. Dad came to check in on me to make sure I was sleeping OK. He woke me because he was worried something was wrong. Apparently, I was lying flat on my back and breathing quite deeply. Like we were this afternoon before our adventure. But more worrying to him was that I was talking in my sleep. He couldn’t make out what I was saying though. Phew!

I told him that everything was OK and that I was dreaming of eating chocolate cake with you guys. Once he understood I was OK he gave me a kiss and a cuddle, turned out the light and then left leaving the door ajar. So, then I yelled out to him to come back and close my door. He looked at me with a startled look and asked if I was sure. I shouted at him a big Yes. I'm a big girl and I like the door closed. I've never asked for the door to be closed before as I've always actually been afraid of the dark, but strangely I'm not afraid anymore! As soon as dad closed the door, I closed my eyes and here I am… again. This magic is sooo cool!"

We all nodded back in agreement. We looked at each other and wondered how Ginger knew Joss's dad had woken her up. Ted then spoke up. The gang kind of looked up to Ted because he was slightly older than us, albeit only by a year.

"So how is this possible? How did you know about Joss's dad and how have we ended up back here" he asked.

"Yeah, how did this happen?" we all chimed in together.

Ginger then spoke. "I can't tell you how, not yet anyway, but I can tell you that you aren't dreaming. This is real! There is nothing stopping you coming here anytime you want; you just have to work out how you did it tonight. You have to work this out for yourselves. Tonight, is to do with your state of mind which is based on alignment. You have reached the power of ONE mind right now, but I can't tell you how you became this way tonight as you will soon enough work this out for yourselves."

Ginger never did answer the question about Joss being woken by her dad and we forgot to ask again. Obviously, we didn't really understand what Ginger was saying at the time about being one, but because she was with us, we thought we did. We thought we could go here anytime we pleased and all we had to do was close our eyes. It didn't take us long to realise our alignment wasn't a case of just closing our eyes.

Ted was the first to ask how much time we had before we would be waking up in our beds to start the next new day. Ginger told us that time here went much faster than in our daily lives.

Then Ginge said with a huge grin on her face "Today/tonight is the start of some amazing adventures together."

We all just looked at each other in total awe. This is something that you dream about or see in the movies. None of us had ever experienced anything as surreal as this, day or night. And yesterday and tonight was the beginning of how our lives changed forever. Everything that we had been taught as truth now seemed to be turned upside down. Our view of the world seemed limited now that we had seen so much more than we even knew existed.

Ginger gave us all a hug and then asked us to join hands again. The same as the first time in the day but this time we were standing and not sitting. Ginger then spoke, "Guys, so we will catch up here on Saturday when we meet at the river again". We all just nodded with huge grins on our faces… as anyone would. Ginger then said goodnight to us, and we all said goodnight back and to each other. I was so excited that any troubles I had seemed a thousand miles away.

Michael and Ted just then disappeared. Ginger looked at the rest of us with a big smile and then said that they were waking up to the new day. She looked at me and as I was about to ask if I was next, I found myself lying in my bed and opening my eyes to a brand-new day. The sun was already shining in all its glory and so was my big cheesy grin.

MUM'S SURPRISE

I had heard adults talking about life changing experiences. I never really knew what they were talking about before but now I knew I did. I had just had a life changing experience thanks to Ginge and I hadn't even hit my teenage years yet. At age 12 I had gone through something I'm sure my parents had never gone through.

There was a knock at my bedroom door and then my mum came in. "Oh, you're awake, good! How did you sleep after all that activity?" mum said. I froze… she knew…? How? Did she come into my room during the night?

I opened my mouth to ask her how she knew but fortunately as my mouth was opening so slowly, she spoke instead. "It was great how you and your friends went to the river yesterday. You came back looking so refreshed. I thought to myself at dinner that you're bound to sleep well tonight. And looking at you now you do look really refreshed. I was a bit surprised though as your togs weren't used and I thought you would have gone for a swim."

Mum gave me a big hug and kiss and then continued. "What would you like to do today? Your dad has gone to work and as your summer break is nearing its end, I thought we could do something together before it is back to school again for you. After a long pause she then asked "Are you OK? Charlie, are you OK?"

I looked at mum and realised I had drifted off into space dreaming about yesterday and last night. "Huh?" I paused and then realised she was starting to look a bit worried. "Yeah I'm OK thanks" I said as quickly as possible hoping that was the right answer as I didn't quite hear her question.

"So, what do you think?" mum said.

"Huh?" I replied wondering what it was she was talking about.

Mum spoke again, "About us doing something special together today?"

"Oh, yeah… OK….. ummm… sounds ah…. grand". I responded slowly whilst I was considering my options for the day.

In reality I wanted to see the gang, but I had to wait till Saturday as agreed. Today was Tuesday. I've not really wished for the summer break days to fly by but now all I wanted was for it to be the weekend. Thinking like this was a bit silly as that meant school was about to start as well.

"So, what would you like to do?" mum asked again. This time she seemed to be looking a bit agitated. I'm not sure why… LOL.

"I want to make something for Ginger. Can we make her a cake or something?" Ginger ate a plant-based diet and I had never baked a cake from plants before. Mum smiled at me then asked when I was seeing Ginger again and I told her Saturday.

"That wont do" mum said with a big smile on her face.

"Why?" I asked and did not get why she was smiling when I couldn't do the only thing I wanted to do.

Mum continued, "1. Because the cake won't keep fresh that long and 2, your dad and I thought we would go away with you on Friday and come back on Sunday. Dad has arranged to take a day off work just so that we can spend some holiday time away from the house together. Before you go back to school and homework gets in the way."

I looked at mum and couldn't believe what was coming out of her mouth. I had just told her about Saturday and here she was changing my plans and with a huge smile on her face.

"Noooooo" I shouted.

"Excuse me?" mum replied looking somewhat surprised and disappointed.

I spoke with an urgent tone and tried not to shout anymore or sound demanding. I didn't want to raise any suspicions. "I need to be here on Saturday. All of us, the gang are catching up on Saturday. We must catch up!" I responded as softly as I could.

"I'm sorry Charlie. Dad and I arranged this trip for us to spend time as a family. We've booked the hotel and everything else. We've not gone away together as a family for a long time because your dad and I have been working. This is our last opportunity for"

I interrupted her which was also a surprise as our family always allowed anyone talking to finish what they said. We weren't allowed to interrupt as this was seen as rude. The rule applied to everyone, children and adults.

"Mum I can't go. You and dad go. I will stay with Ginge. This Saturday is really important to me." I had cut my mum off mid-sentence, but this was one of those moments that needed some firefighting and this fire I urgently needed to put out.

Mum got up and looked at me with a really disappointed face. I could see she was upset, and I didn't like upsetting her because my mum was really cool. I loved her so much, but this Saturday was one of the most important days in my life. And I couldn't tell her about it because it was a secret. A secret that I couldn't tell a soul, not even my own mother. This left me feeling a bit guilty also.

Mum then spoke; "Let's talk it out over dinner tonight as a family."

"OK" I said.

"Well I can think of two things we can do today. We could go shopping and get you some new gear. Or we could go to the SPCA and do some volunteer work. I know how much you love animals." Mum said the last bit with a warm gentle smile. It was true. I loved animals. I loved their little eyes, their little mouths, the silky touch of their fur, their cute whiskers that make them look like they are either smiling or frowning. I loved animals and hoped that when I was an adult that my job would involve helping animals in some way or another.

We did go to the SPCA but I was considered too young to help with the animals and so they gave us some rags to take home to cut up for the animal beds. After the SPCA mum and I went to the river for a swim. Although the day was just as sunny as yesterday the river wasn't sparkling like it was before our purple adventure. Whilst we were swimming and splashing each other I so wanted to tell mum about the purple forest but of all secrets that kids try to keep, this was one that I had to keep to myself.

When dad came home, we had a long chat over dinner. I managed to convince dad that it was best I stay behind so that mum and he could have a romantic time away. I didn't really know what romantic meant but I had heard mum on the phone saying how romantic dad was and that they hadn't had a chance to have many romantic experiences together. I knew I must look the word up on the internet one day. Anyway, luck was on my side and mum and dad agreed so long as I had somewhere safe to stay. I couldn't eat my dinner fast enough so that it would be over, and then I could ring Ginger and ask to stay at her house.

When dinner was finished, I rang Ginger and Rachel spoke with my mum and the deal was sealed. I would be spending two nights with Ginger. Ye-hah!

PARENTS GO TO TIME-OUT

For each night that went past none of us met up again in our sleep. We didn't know why we couldn't go back when we talked about it on the phone, so it seemed we had to wait until Saturday to find out. But now it was Friday morning; my overnight bag was packed, and I'd finished my breakfast. I wasn't that hungry but to keep the peace I finished my corn flakes. I'd finished brushing my teeth and almost finished combing my wavy hair when dad yelled out my name and asked if I was ready. I came racing down the stairs with my favourite blue denim overnight bag, raced out the front door and hopped straight into the car. I finished brushing my hair and then put my brush in my bag, put my seat belt on and patiently waited for mum and dad to lock up the house and get in the car. Within minutes we were on our way. It was a 10 minute drive to Ginger's house that seemed to take an hour. I sat in the back seat feeling like I was about to burst at the seams with excitement.

As soon as we arrived at Ginger's, mum, dad and I got out of the car. Our parents spoke with each other and then my mum and dad came over to me and each gave me a big hug. Mum looked like she was going to cry but then her face suddenly changed to a big warm smile. With the bright sunlight I could see wrinkles near the corners of her eyes all shaped upwards like the smile on her mouth. I hadn't noticed wrinkles on mum before. Dad looked at mum and winked and said, "Come on let's go before Charlie changes her mind."

Yeah right, as if I would change my mind. Mum and dad drove off, we waved back and forth to each other, and I stopped waving once I could no longer see our car. I started to feel a little sad as I felt that changes were in the air. I felt like I was saying goodbye for the first of many times to come. Goodbye to being a child and suddenly realising that mum and dad, like most adults are just grown-up children. That parents still need to experience fun in life just like us children. It means they get to do things that make them happy, and I guess they also need time-out from the huge age gap between parents and children. Basically, they want fun just like us kids as well.

I looked at my watch and realised it was now 10:00am on Friday. Ginger and I had three days and two nights together and we would see the whole gang on Saturday. I felt really happy inside and excited. I was wondering what the next few days had in store especially as this was the first time I had ever stayed overnight at Gingers.

Ginger's mum came over to me, put her arm around my shoulders, looked me in the eye and said let's go inside and put your beautiful bag away. I looked at her and smiled as this was my favourite bag and she noticed it. Ginger held my hand and we skipped down the hallway to her room with her mum following close behind.

We went into Ginger's room which was just amaz.....ing. Wow, it is similar colours to the forest! It was blue and purple based on various shades of the two colours. The blues made the room look kinda cold but the splashes of shades of purple gave the room a warm feeling. I was shown my bed and put my bag in the wardrobe.

GINGER'S HOME

Not hippies as such although I'm sure some people would think so. I think a hippie might be someone with long hair who dresses in long flowing rainbow clothing, maybe?

Ginger's mum Rachel liked to be called exactly that, Rachel. There were no formalities because of age gaps. She said she didn't call me Miss Charlie and I wasn't allowed to call her Aunty Rachel. This perspective seemed strange although she justified this by saying "As I wasn't her niece then she wasn't my Aunty as we weren't blood related." Then she smiled and winked and said "We are much more than that." I didn't know what she meant by being more than that at the time, but it wasn't too long down the track before I found out.

Anyhuu, Ginge and I would normally chat about school and clothes and stuff like that when we got together, but since 'the event' I wanted our topic of conversation to change.

"You want to hear more don't you?" Ginge said. One didn't have to be a rocket scientist to work that out I thought followed by a quiet giggle.

And before I could speak Ginge said "I thought you loved science." "I'm so sorry" she quickly said. "I didn't mean to hear your thoughts, sometimes I forget to tune out. We have a rule not to eavesdrop as it is rude and it is abusing our gifts, so I'm really sorry. I've not done this before with you. I think my excitement about sharing with you has momentarily got the better of me."

I didn't know what to think, especially as I wasn't sure if I should now anyway... LOL. So I said "Ginge it's OK. I know you are sincere and the last person I know of who would eavesdrop."

Ginge started to speak, "OK, so tell me if I'm wrong on any of this. I think you want to hear about a few things

1. How had we got to the land of purple?
2. Why I knew about the interruptions in your own homes when you were in your own bedrooms?
3. Where is the land of purple?
4. What does all of this mean?
5. When will we be able to travel back there, as you've not managed to get back since?"

Ginge paused and then said, "Does that sum your questions up?"

I looked at Ginge so intently I felt like my eyes would pop out of my head. "Yes please Ginge I want to hear all of that."

Ginge said she couldn't answer all of the questions now as the answers weren't quite black and white, but she would answer them over time and with the others. She said though that Rachel (her mum) and she thought that I had some hidden talents that would allow me to understand quickly. I just knew there was a reason that Ginge and I connected so easily which had allowed us to become instant best friends.

Ginge continued to speak "To answer the question of how we got there. You know when you learn to ride a bike you have to pay full attention to what you are doing and then once you know how then you no longer have to put in any effort? It's like when you concentrate on something you are right here, right now, in the present, in the moment being presented to you. This presence is also known as being fully conscious in the moment. There is no time to daydream. To daydream means you don't know what is going on right in front of you because, well, because your mind is elsewhere, it is in the daydream. The daydream has taken your mind back to something that happened in the past, or you are dreaming about something in the future that hasn't happened yet. To be thinking of the past or the future means we aren't fully conscious as we have let ourselves be taken out of the present moment.

So, the way we got to the purple Forrest was to take ourselves out of the present moment which is what we do when we fall asleep. We let our consciousness relax enough to allow the start of the transition into what we call our dream state. But you weren't in a dream state when we met at the forest, you were just relaxed enough to allow a state change. So, you could still be aware of everything and yet move out of your current reality as you know it, i.e., in your bedroom on the verge of falling asleep or relaxed through breathing when we were holding hands down at the river."

"So, what you are saying Ginge is that we weren't physically in the purple Forrest, we were still in our beds or at the stream. Our minds though connected which allowed us to see each other in what appeared to be a physical form. Arghh... Which I don't get.... how can I be in bed and in the purple Forrest?"

Ginge replied "The same as when you daydream Charlie! Your body is physically not in the daydream, but you see yourself as if you were completely in the dream. Where I took you is real Charlie, BUT I could only take you this way first. Being ready to sleep or relaxed through breathing meant I didn't need to compete with your thoughts, so I could take you there without your body and without your mind freaking out. Anyway, let's spend the rest of the day having some earthly fun like kids do and we can talk more tomorrow with the others. Agree?"

"Yeah sounds good" I said half wanting to talk more and the other half just wanting to play like normal kids do.

Knock knock knock.... It was Rachel's mum knocking at Ginger's door and she said with a smile "Ladies, will you be so kind to come and join me for lunch?"

Ginge and I had sandwiches for lunch and then spent the rest of the day playing, singing on the karaoke machine and climbing the trees in the back yard. The day went so quickly and was full of so much fun that Saturday was now just around the corner.

When night came by it was time to start winding down for the evening. Just as well as I was exhausted. I hadn't had so much fun in ages. Before I went to bed Mum rang to check in on me and also said how much fun they were having. It seems that time out for us all was working out just perfectly. □

Once we were all tucked up in bed I said, "Ginge, will we go there tonight?"

"Not tonight, Charlie we need our energy for tomorrow with the rest of the gang. Night Charlie!"

"Night Ginge!" And then I closed my eyes with my big, huge cheesy grin on my face from all this awesome excitement in my life.

SATURDAY

Ginge and I skipped all the way to the river with a few handstands and cartwheels along the way. The rest of our gang were already there and waiting with big eager grins on their faces. Except for Michael, their grins were so wide I'm sure I could have counted all their teeth.

Ginge went over to Michael and asked if he was OK because although Michael had a small grin, there was something not quite right which of course Ginge picked up on. You could see he was a bit taken aback by her asking and he said a little defensively with his arms now crossed against his chest, "Yeah, I'm OK! Why?"

Ginge said in a soft voice, that we could barely hear her "Michael, I know it has been a hard week with what has been going on for you but just remember not to own anyone else's issues." Ginge had seen what had happened to Michael during this last week because of her magic. Then Michael shared with us how his father had yelled at him telling him how useless he was, and he would never amount to anything.

Ginge went on to explain to all of us whilst mostly looking at Michael what projecting was and that his father wasn't feeling good about himself. When people feel insecure, they sometimes try whatever they can to make themselves feel better. His father didn't realise that his anger he had towards his company was being directed at his family. The anger he had at his company was being taken out on Michael which of course made Michael feel like crap. Ginge explained projecting like this probably made his father feel worse for hurting his son that he loved.

Ginge went on to say, "When someone is hurting, sometimes they hurt those that are close to them to try and feel better themselves. It never works though."

"Looks like it worked for him" said Michael looking like he was about to cry. "And why hurt those that love you? What has he got to feel insecure about anyway? It's not him who has the stress of doing homework each night and studying to pass tests."

"Your father has lost his job which is why he is angry at his company. He doesn't know how he is going to find another job," said Joss.

"What? Far out man, how do you know that Ginge as I've not heard anything?"

"Because Michael I can see things, it's one of the gifts I have been given. That doesn't excuse your dad's behaviour towards you but explains that he has a lot on his mind that he needs to sort out. When some people are very stressed, they struggle to show love and kindness to others. He just needs to accept that the job loss isn't to do with him, it is to do with the company he works for."

"Like I said, far out man, your magic rocks!" Michael exclaimed. "I will now have to act surprised when I find out but, in the meantime, when I'm at home I think I will spend more time in my room studying for my tests."

Ginge replied, "Just remember not to take anything personally because when someone else speaks it is their opinion, not yours. And don't worry about the future because it's not here yet. If you stay focused on the present, which is the here and now, you will see you have the support of your family and your friends."

"Friends" asked Michael.

"Us" said Ginge with a big warm smile, and then she continued. "Whenever you feel down remember it is only temporary and everything changes - good times and bad times will always visit us and then they leave us to make room for new experiences, new times. That is how we learn, how we grow, how we become wise."

We all looked at Michael with big beautiful soft smiles. After what seemed like a very long pause he said "You know what, I actually feel better already."

All he needed was our love and that is what we gave him. We all went up and gave him a big group hug and then, as if by instinct, we sat down in our little circle and held hands and closed our eyes and focused on our breath.

When we opened our eyes, we were back in the land of purple. Ginge looked at all of us and said in a quiet voice "Who wants to take a look around?" No answer was needed as we all just stood up and then started to follow Ginge.

After 5mins Ginger stopped, turned around and looked at all of us. Without opening her mouth, she asked us if we could hear her and if so to reply back the same way; to use our minds. All of us could hear each other when we replied “Yes” with our minds. And of course, again we couldn’t quite wipe the grins off our faces when we realised that we could speak and listen to each other without having to open our mouths. Ginge carried on, “This place becomes way more magical if we don’t speak but just communicate through our mind. If you use someone’s name before you speak then that sentence will only be heard by them. Try it Charlie.”

I concentrated with my eyes closed, and then in my mind asked Joss if she liked my shoes. Joss looked at me and at my shoes and replied back with her mind “Charlie, I like your shoes very much”. In my mind I then said “Everyone, Joss likes my shoes” and the rest of the gang all looked at my shoes and started laughing.... in silence of course.

Ginge told us to go and check out the forest for ourselves and so we did. We all went off in different directions and I’m sure none of us had any idea what to expect next, I know I didn’t.

MY MAGIC

"Hello Charlie" the voices in my head were soft, calming and although not recognisable they sounded friendly. I looked around and couldn't see anyone, expecting the rest of our gang to jump out and surprise me. I was frozen in fear as I couldn't see who was talking to me.

"Charlie there is nothing to fear when you are surrounded by love." Again, I looked around but this time with a more inquisitive mind than with caution.

"Who is there?" I asked again with my mind.

"You call us trees when you are in your own environment so let's use that name whilst you are here in our home."

"Oh my gosh, trees can talk?" I asked, once again feeling like my eyes were about to pop out of my head from the amount of surprise on my face.

The trees continued to speak, "Yes, we have that ability here because of the silence. When we are all silent, we can hear more than we realise. Nature has so much to say but humans only seem to listen to each other, if they even do that."

I replied back "That's because where I come from humans are the only ones who have mastered how to speak languages. Nature doesn't talk and animals have very limited ways of communicating."

The trees spoke again, "Maybe that is the way it is for humans where you come from, maybe. Humans have a way to keep themselves occupied that they seldom stay quiet enough to listen to what is really going on. And if they are on their own, they use devices to stop them from listening to silence. Anyway, enough of your world we want you to learn about ours. Charlie, we know that you are old enough to start questioning what you have been told by humans. You are at an age now where you can start to find out your own truths. We that live here are ancient. We used to share the same lands as you but if we had all stayed, we wouldn't have survived so we left to find our own paradise which we share with some humans who can be trusted. There are so many different animals and species here, but you can't see them yet as they have chosen to blend in with the environment. Humans haven't been the kindest to many of us when we tried to co-exist by sharing the land you come from. This means it takes a while for the others here to trust before they decide to make themselves known."

I was about to ask how the trees know all this and then the trees continued to talk.

"We trees share our knowledge through our root system, we share pain, joy, laughter, wisdom and insight. It is our root system that allows us to communicate with each other. Think of it as our underground network. Our roots connect with each other which makes us stronger and allows us to pass our love and wisdom on to the seedlings who can then grow and become mature like us.

Charlie, we saw that you were impressed with being able to talk with your mind which adults call telepathy, so if you think talking with your mind is quite incredible then try this. Put your arms out to each side of your body with your palms facing the ground." I did as they advised. The trees then said, "Good, now put your palms facing up towards the sky."

"Oh my gosh I'm slowly lifting off the ground and I can't seem to stop" I said. I could hear the trees gently laughing which I responded to with a very slight and nervous smile.

Then one of the large branches of the tree in front of me grabbed me and held me and then said, "Well done Charlie! Now to go up, keep your palms up and to go down put your palms towards the ground. If you want to turn whilst in the air clench the fist of the direction you want to go. If you want to stop reach both your palms out in front of you. And whenever you land back on your feet always say thank you as gratitude shows a sign of respect."

"You mean like when I say thank you to the sun for shining so I can go outside and play" I said.

"Yes, and on days that you can't go out and play because of the weather you should also say thank you. The weather has many gifts. The rain waters us, the wind helps clear the air, the cold gives people time for rest and rejuvenation. And the warmth, as you say allows you to go outside and play. Oh, and one more thing, think of us trees as your angels as we will always be looking out for you. To connect with us where you come from then just give us a hug. We will feel the tree hug from here Charlie. And each time you visit us here then just picture us in your mind before you start talking with us. We will always be here for you watching over you like God loves and watches over you. It's time now for you to join up with your friends as Ginger is about to call you back. All of you have different talents here and yours is to fly. See you soon Charlie!"

And they really did stop talking as I could no longer hear them. Just momentary silence. Wow, wow and wow. Before I had time to think again about the trees, I did hear Ginge in my mind calling us back.

I started to head back, skipping along as I was so happy but then I realised I had no idea which way was back. I started walking, then running and then stopped suddenly. I froze again, this time from panic as I couldn't seem to find my way back to the group. I couldn't see any clearings, just trees and more trees. How was I going to get out of here? I sat down by a small tree that had a skinny straight trunk with hardly any branches. The few branches it did have were loaded with purple and lilac leaves, and then I couldn't help but bury my head in my hands as I burst into tears.

The tree I sat next to reached out to me and softly said "Charlie, use your flight. Lift yourself up into the air so that you can look down and see the clearing where the others will meet you."

Suddenly my tears stopped as I felt a bit of an idjit as I had just been taught how to fly and now I needed to be told again how to use my magic. I had been so scared that I completely forgot to talk with the trees neither did I think to reach out and speak with Ginger.

I gave that tree a big hug, remembered to say thank you and then lifted my arms out to the side of my body and then put my palms facing up. I lifted off with the biggest smile ever. I was grinning so hard my jaws and cheeks started to really hurt. I started to move up and around.

I could now see everything more clearly and then I saw the meeting area with Joss, Michael and Ginge standing around waiting.

As I came down to land by them Joss and Michael looked at me in utter surprise. Ginge put her finger against her mouth to tell us to be quiet as she could hear something. Sure enough Ted seemed to appear out of nowhere. Oh my gosh, had he been invisible?

Before we could even try to share stories Ginger put her hands out and then got us to sit in our circle. We closed our eyes, automatically said thank you, listened for the river and then we heard it. When we opened our eyes we were back in our own environment where the only thing that was still purple was the colour of Joss's top. It was now dusk and getting close to dinner time. We all looked at Ginge and then she smiled and said out aloud "School on Monday."

We looked at her puzzled. How could she talk about school after where we had just been? We've learnt more today than any school could teach us. Ginge continued, "So this is only to be talked about here with each other. It's too dangerous to talk about this anywhere else. Not even with your parents. I know you have lots to say, and we will, but for now we have to wait for tonight when you are about to sleep."

We smiled knowing that tonight we could continue from the comfort of our beds. Which was just as well because some older kids had just arrived on their bikes, and they didn't look like they wanted to be friendly.

The biggest one said, "What are you kids doing here this late, shouldn't you be at home sleeping?" They all started laughing at us whilst looking at us and then making sideways glances at each other. I didn't find what they said funny, in fact I just wanted to get home so we could eat dinner and then meet up in our sleep.

Ginge spoke up rather confidently and said to them “Hi, we are just leaving but it is a cool spot here by the river.” Just then the river started to make weird sounds, like rocks were swishing around in it or like someone had thrown rocks into it. As the older kids got closer to the river their laughter stopped. They actually started to look nervous or scared. Ginge looked at us and nodded as if to say that was our opportunity to go. Had the river just helped us to get away from the bullies?

“I’ve got to go as I need to get back for dinner” Joss said aloud.

“Me too” we shouted in unison. And then apart from Ginge and myself, the others went their separate ways and we left the older kids still staring at the river. I ran with Ginge back to her house where her mum was opening the door just as we arrived at the doorstep. How did she know we were arriving at that moment?

DINNER IS SERVED!

Rachel had dinner ready for us on the table. Can you guess what was on our plates? Purple cabbage with purple eggplant, carrots and potato stew. Our dinner was purple. I looked at the dinner and then looked at Ginge and then at Rachel.

Rachel said “There is an organic farmer down the road who sells fruit and veges in their original colour. Man changed colours of some veges a long time ago, so these here are the original colours. For example, man made the carrot orange and the potato white. I think they taste the same as the coloured versions but as you can see the purple colours are all really, well, rather pretty. So shall we hold hands and show our gratitude for the food that is before us. Thank you God for the food that is before us. Thank you for bringing Charlie into our home so that she may experience your love in our home. Thank you for taking care of Luke whilst he is living your light and love away from our home. Amen.” Ginge said Amen and so I did too. It was my first time.

“Who is Luke?” I asked.

"My dad" said Ginge. "He has been away for about six months but we get to talk whenever he can. He is spending most of his time in the Amazon trying to protect the rainforest as they say trees are the lungs of the earth and most of the trees are in the Amazon."

"Let's eat," said Rachel. And so we did.

Later that night as we were settling down to go to sleep, I meant to ask Ginge about her dad Luke. The lungs of the earth sounded like that involved my time here on earth, but with the day's excitement I completely forgot. I also wanted to ask about what happened with the river when the older boys on their bikes turned up but with one yawn my eyes started to close for sleep. And most of all I wanted to know where it was that we go but we both must have drifted off at the same time as once again we were back with our faithful gang.

Ginge started off the telepathic conversation. "I have a few gifts as I've been doing this most of my life. You all have been given your own unique gifts for now from this beautiful forest but as time passes and you work together in love and peace with each other you will be able to access each other's gifts. This is because we are all connected. We are all One. And one important factor to never forget, because the trees want peace then the only way your magic will work is when you are full of love. If you are angry your magic will never work, even if you desperately need it to, even if your life depends on it. Negative emotions stop miracles from happening and your gifts are miracles. For your magic to work you will have to let go your anger or sadness or whatever it is that stops you from smiling."

Joss asked "When you say we are all One do you mean us five are connected? That we are special just like you?"

Ginge replied "All beings are connected. So yes, we too are connected but the purple forest allows us to connect on a much deeper level than most humans can. So don't accidentally limit yourself nor others. If you want to be as free as I am then you need to see love and light. What you think about and give emotion to is what you attract. This is a universal truth, and this purple forest is here to teach you this just as much as your own lives will. For what you learn here you will take with you so long as you are at peace and have faith. Questions later though when your body is awake, for now let's share what we learnt. Charlie do you want to go first?"

I started to tell them how the trees had taught me to fly.

"Wait a moment" said Ginge. "Do you want to tell them or show them?"

"What do you mean by showing them?" I asked.

Ginge replied, "I mean do you want to take them back to the past when you were with the trees?"

I was about to say yes as it sounded like another really cool bit of magic when I remembered getting lost and crying, and well, I wasn't wanting to share that. I like people to think I'm really brave and so I said, "I will tell them."

I mentioned that the trees had made this place their sanctuary as there was not much of a sanctuary for them anymore on earth. I mentioned how not only could they talk but that they were also connected by their root structure and that they used this root structure to gain knowledge over the generations. This knowledge was within all of the trees and when one tree learnt then they all learnt. One experience was an immediate shared experience and because of this the trees had quicky learned wisdom. They said they use to move about a long time ago but they gave up their freedom of movement so they could truly learn wisdom. It had cost them the ability to escape danger the way we know to, but in the process, they had become closer to each other. They said that nature has a way of self-generating if people aren't around to destroy it.

Michael piped up and asked, "Are you saying these trees came here as we humans had destroyed most of their home on earth?"

"Yeah, I guess" I replied.

Ginge piped up and said "We are all one, when we love, everyone gains, and when we destroy, we all suffer the loss. We can't expect our actions to have no consequences. We may not see the consequences immediately, but we will see them at some stage through our connected souls. Michael, you go next. Tell us about your experience here."

It kinda felt like we were rushing but I guess we had to get through our stories before it was time to wake up and start the new day.

THE REST OF THE MAGIC

"Wow where do I begin" said Michael before he continued. "I was wandering along when the trees spoke with me also. But they never said anything about a sanctuary. The more I think about what they said and showed me, I guess they did imply that this was their last resort. I didn't realise the problem was because us humans had destroyed so much of their habitat."

We all looked eagerly at Michael waiting to tell us and after a long pause he finally continued.

"I can see into the past and future. The trees told me to pick a year, any year and I would be able to see how everything looked based on the year I chose. For example, I could see how everything looked when I was a kid."

Before he had a chance to continue, we piped up and said with a giggle "You still are a kid Michael."

Michael looked at us with a smirk and then continued, "Or I can see into our future. So out of curiosity for my first time, I chose to go forwards not backwards. But I didn't get to spend much time looking as it seems I spent most of my time talking with the trees and learning how to use this magic." Then Michael started to talk faster "We have to change. I saw myself and I didn't recognise myself nor my surroundings."

Ginge interrupted Michael and asked him if he wanted to tell us or show us.

Michael quickly responded - "Let's show them."

Ginge then said "OK to do this we need to have our hands in a palm to palm position, keep your fingers straight and all look towards Michael with your eyes closed whilst he shows us his memory."

In our circle we did as Ginge had instructed. It wasn't long before Michael took us to the river, to our river that we played in and had our picnics. Nothing looked like it does now. There was no river, it was all dried up. There was no grass and no trees to climb in. It was really dusty and everything seemed brown and somehow no longer felt alive. Michael dropped his hands from the circle, and we no longer saw the future of our river. The rest of us then dropped our hands to our sides.

Michael continued through his telepathy. "When I opened my eyes to be back here the trees told me this was our future if humans didn't change. What we just saw was real given the current path humans are taking." Michael took a really long pause and then yelled "Did you see that there were no trees!" We looked at each other nodding and then back at Michael as he continued. "On earth right now, trees are green. The trees said it was a symbol of love as we are all connected. Plant and animal life is **a part** of us not **apart** from us. We humans and the planet need plant life to survive. We show our love to nature by taking care of the planet and nature loves us back by making everything that we need to live. What the trees told Charlie is what I saw. Everything was just mud, there was nothing to soak up the water. Everything was just a muddy or dusty brown colour. Then I asked the trees was there any hope and they said your parents had a song that they listened to by someone as the same name as me which was called the Earth Song. They said that song as powerful as it was, wasn't enough to make humans change. I don't know the song but when I wake up, I'm going to look it up on the search engine and play it on my computer."

We all looked at each other and couldn't believe what the trees had said. That there was no hope. Tears looked like they were about to start in Joss's eyes.

Michael saw our concern and continued in a really calm voice. "They explained where there is hope there is fear and people don't do anything when they live on either of the two. One feeds off the other. Hope is just a positive aspect of the word fear and neither words are about taking action now. They said we have to have faith that humans will try and do the right thing now. Right now! Faith allows us to have faith in our own actions and then we actively do what is right for everyone. You know... God helps those that help themselves. The trees said the universe is watching us and we have to stop destroying the planet. They said we need to act with love and by living from the heart not only will we be looked after but so will the planet. They said most adults have lost their way. They have closed their hearts because they lost faith in themselves to make a difference. But we humans are the only ones who can save (he then continued after a very long pause), ourselves."

Joss piped up and said "Yes the planet needs us to love it for what we love will love us back and what we unnecessarily destroy will ultimately destroy us. My mum has a favourite song from when she was a teenager by The Black Eyed Peas called *Where is the love?* The song makes so much sense to me now. I feel like we are being told that we can only save ourselves through love."

“That was profound” said Michael.

Joss replied, “Yes the trees taught me the ability to see consequences of actions. They told me I can use this to guide us in helping to make the right choices when we are unsure what to do. Which I think is pretty cool. You know how many times you wonder what to do, well I have the ability to see the consequences. I can see into a crystal ball which I think is the best thing ever, although it doesn’t stop us from changing the outcome to something that isn’t in our best interests. They said although we always say we want to operate from love or kindness we seem to struggle and justify why we can’t be kind. For example, down at the stream today when the bullies were picking on us, I didn’t feel very loving towards them. I was still scared and feared them. And I had just been taught by the trees as to why we should use love and kindness and then in reality I was angry with the bullies and scared of them.”

“Sounds fair enough to me, why should we love or even trust bullies” Ted asked.

“Because Ted,” Joss paused for a bit then continued “they aren’t really bullies. They probably haven’t experienced love, so they are just doing what they know. How can we be angry with them if they don’t know any better? When we know, when we **really** know, and the trees emphasised ‘REALLY’, when we really know better, we act accordingly. When we react, we become like the bullies and all that does is justify their behaviour. You know the saying our parents taught us that two wrongs don't make a right. It was awesome how Ginge diffused the situation today. We didn’t have to fight; we were able to peacefully get away. Ginge acted with love.”

Ginge butted in and said with a wink "OK Joss, tell us how you used your crystal ball today. That's if you have finished for now Michael, I mean Mr Jackson."

Joss started telling us about her experience. "Well actually the trees showed me the bullies at the river. I saw it all before it actually happened to us. Which is why I couldn't do anything because I couldn't believe I was having real déjà vu, like we have talked about in class. The trees showed me the bullies at the river and they showed me my response and told me as this is my first time to see consequences to let Ginge handle it. I wanted to fight back as much as I knew I wouldn't win because I'm so small and as the trees explained, I wasn't responding with love. The trees said most of the mess this world is in is because instead of coming from love we act from fear. We want to hurt those that hurt us, an eye for an eye, rather than stepping back and stopping this awful cycle of wanting to hurt each other. And in the process, everyone is hurting, and no one wins, especially the planet."

Ted asked, "So how come you still wanted to hurt the bullies after you saw it was the wrong thing to do?"

"Hey, I've only just learnt this, and change is really hard. I guess because I was scared, and fear got the better of my thoughts. And how many times have you tried to change something about yourself only to keep doing the stuff you want to change. You know I have a friend that eats peanut butter by the spoonful. He swears that each time he does it, it will be the last, but sure enough when he goes to study for a test, he gets out a spoon and the jar of peanut butter."

"Yeah, I can totally relate to that," said Ted. "I let my emotions get the better of me sometimes and tell myself I won't get angry when something doesn't go my way and then when I do get angry, I think my body has been invaded by a 4 year old."

We all started laughing with Ted as we could totally relate to not acting our age sometimes.

Ted piped up again "So it must be my turn."

"Can you turn invisible?" I asked in an excited voice.

"Not quite Charlie" said Ted. The trees taught me how I can look like my environment. So to you I look invisible but actually I'm not, I just can blend in so well that you can't see me. And that's it!"

"How will you use this gift?" asked Joss.

"I haven't figured that out yet. The trees told me I would know when to use it. I can only use it in the real world as it has no use here. I was almost going to use it down at the river today to see what the older kids were talking about but in the end realised there was no need."

Ginge interrupted and said "See you guys at school." And before I could say anything else I was back in Ginger's room waking up to lunchtime on Sunday. I had slept so long that the morning had passed me by. Luckily, I wasn't at home as mum would surely have woken me up before we could have finished telling our stories.

WE ARE ONE

Rachel's mum knocked on the door of Ginger's room before she entered. Ginge and Rachel looked into each other's eyes and then Rachel sat down on my bed.

"Morning Charlie," said Rachel.

I sat up in bed and was about to reply before I interrupted myself with a big yawn. I wasn't feeling well but I didn't know why.

Rachel then held my hands and said in a soft and gentle voice, "Charlie your parents are OK" and then Rachel paused for what felt like such a long time before continuing, "they have been in an accident and are in hospital. They would love to see you today and have asked if you could also continue to stay here until they are released back home which should be in just a few days' time. I told them we would love to have you stay here for as long as it takes for them to recover. And I said we would take you to the hospital to see them during visiting hours which starts in about two hours time. So when you and Ginge are ready come downstairs for lunch and then we will go to the hospital."

I just sat there and slowly nodded back in a yes response. I realised I wasn't feeling well because I had a sinking feeling in my stomach and this information about the accident was the sinking feeling. Somehow, I knew that something was wrong.

Rachel smiled at me and then said "Everything is going to be OK and I can see you are being really brave about this. I will go now and leave you two to get ready."

We got dressed in silence and after we were both dressed I looked at Ginge and she confirmed what her mum had just said, "It's true, everything is going to be OK. Your parents will be home soon. But if you don't believe me…"

Just then I got a text on my phone and it was from Joss.

I read the text out aloud to Ginge. "I'm sorry to hear the news about your parents, so just to let you know I've seen that they will be OK. Look forward to lunch break at school tomorrow."

Ginge looked at me and said with a big warm smile "See I told you so!"

Then another text came in and it was from Michael "Charlie just to let you know I woke with a weird feeling in my stomach and didn't know why. I asked Ginge and she said that your parents had been in an accident on their way home. So, I went to your house a week from today and you were there with your parents. All is good! Catch u at school tomorrow."

Then another text, this time from Ted. "Hi Charlie, don't know why I had a funny feeling in my tummy when I woke but when I texted Ginge she told me about your parents. I cycled to the hospital and used my new magic. I only was seen once or twice whilst I was practicing my gift, a bit scary aye, but just to let you know the records show that your parents are OK to be released in a few days' time. See you at school tomorrow."

I looked intently at Ginge and then said "Is this what you mean by the power of one?"

Ginge then did a big star jump on her bed and yelled out a big "YES.

You get it. We knew you would."

"We?" I asked.

"Mum and I knew that you were special like me, you just haven't had the opportunity before to let your magic really start to develop. Being here and living the way we do will show you some of what you are capable of."

I started to slowly ask Ginge my next question as I was trying not to get angry. "Ginge, if you knew my parents were in an accident why didn't you stop it from happening and why didn't you tell me?"

I didn't realise how upset I was at hearing the news and yet I shouldn't be upset because everything was going to be OK. I should actually be happy that everything is OK and more than that, I should be thrilled that we have gifts we can use here, outside of the purple forest. So why was I still upset?

"Hey Charlie, please don't be like that. I can't stop things from happening. No one should have the power to do that because we don't know what the consequences would be no matter how much we may not want something to happen. There is a reason for everything. What we can change are our own actions. We can only change ourselves. Joss can see things in the future but she can't stop the future from happening. What Joss can do is change how she responds to a situation, she can respond instead of react."

Ginge paused for what seemed like forever but I didn't say a thing as I was feeling guilty for saying what I did. "Charlie I did know before mum came into the room. I picked up on you not feeling well but you were still sleeping. Then the guys texted me and then, well, you know. We all care Charlie about you and about each other. This is what love is. Love is caring, and being there for each other, and well, this is us being here for you." Ginge said the last bit with a big beautiful smile.

I leapt out of bed and gave Ginge a big hug. She responded back with the same. We started choking from hugging each other so tight. Next thing we were giggling like schoolgirls do when happiness and friendship collide.

After lunch Rachel took us to the hospital. As it was such a long drive from their house Ginge and I sat in the back of the car having a telepathic conversation about what our first day back at school would be like. Whenever we said anything funny and giggled out aloud Rachel would look at us with a smile through her rear vision mirror.

LOVE IS ALL THERE IS

In the hospital, mum and dad were in separate wards as men and women can't be in the same area. We went to my mum first and Rachel and Ginge waited at the door until after all the hugs and kisses.

Mum said with tears in her eyes "We were very lucky to come out of this with a few scratches. I love you so much Charlie and the doctors have said that we will be able to go home in a few days."

I tried to act surprised hearing that they would be home soon given the rest of the gang had already told me that morning. So, I just said "I love you too mum and I can't wait for us to be together again." The last thing I wanted to do was get into a situation I wouldn't know how to get out of. Telling mum that I knew she was fine would just lead to all sorts of questions. And I've found that silence is best when one is unsure of what to say. Opening my mouth unnecessarily could get me into all sorts of trouble down the track.

After lots of chit chat about each other's weekends and discussing how to get my stuff from the house for school and then more hugs and kisses we went off to see my dad.

There were four other men in the same room as dad and dad was the same as mum. Dad had tears in his eyes and was full of tight hugs, so tight I thought I would start choking again like I did with Ginge. He didn't seem to care about crying in front of the other men, which I thought made him cool.

Dad then explained what mum couldn't. That the back of the car was crushed but the front was fine. He didn't say anymore because he started crying and held me like he didn't want to let me go. I finally understood. If I had been with them and the accident had still taken place, I would have been crushed.

Well would you try and digest that news. I would have ceased to be. I wouldn't be talking to you now, well not like this anyway. And do ghost books exist?

I finally realised what Ginger meant by not changing anything in the past because we don't know the repercussions, the consequences. I wasn't sure how to feel now. If I hadn't gone to stay with Ginge my life would be different, worst case I could be pushing up daisies. Joss never mentioned the car to me nor did Ginge. Did either of them know? But then did it matter? Ginge told me that we have to be in the present, to be in the moment being presented right here, right now. And right now, I am alive. I am loved. I am surrounded by love in every direction. I don't feel like this every day. In fact, on some days, I don't feel much at all but today I realised how precious life is. Not just for me, the person living it, but for those we live and share our lives with. Wow, now I feel like a really old wise person, someone who is at least 20. I am alive, I can fly and I'm like a cat with nine lives. So, with everything being so good, why do I still feel a sadness inside me?

After we left the hospital, we went to my house and got my stuff for the week. I was planning to go home on Wednesday, the day mum and dad would be home from hospital, but just in case I decided to pack for the week. Rachel helped me as I didn't really know what I would need. Mum use to help me get ready for school so it was nice of Rachel to help me out.

Before we left the house Rachel sat me down on the couch and asked me how I was. She looked at me with such a serious look that I just started crying. I don't know where the tears came from, but they wouldn't stop. I was sobbing so loudly I could hardly hear anything else. Rachel just held me in her arms and said "Tears on the outside means they can't hide on the inside." So, I just kept crying and she just kept holding me.

I soon realised my nose had started to run quite a bit and instead of feeling sad I started to feel a bit embarrassed. My sobbing slowed down as I didn't have anything to blow my nose with. And by now my nose was really running, more than the tears from my eyes. I was worried I would get snot all over Rachel's cardigan. Although it was green maybe she wouldn't notice. She looked at me and said, "It's ok Charlie, that's what washing machines are for." She then nodded a Yes before I could ask whether she too could read my mind.

Rachel explained that her gift was there when it was meant to be there. She couldn't do it often, only when it helped a situation. Rachel then explained that a lot of people have this gift, they just need to listen more for it to work. I didn't realise what she meant until years later when I learned through experience that we were given two ears and one mouth for a reason, lol.

I heard that love is being there for others. What adults call being of service to others and at this time I felt I was surrounded by love. Everyone was there for me, when I needed it. Rachel had explained that life isn't always like this. People get caught up in their lives that they can forget each other but right now no one was forgetting me. Everyone I wanted in my little life was there for me.

I am part of The Faithful Five and this is the best thing I have ever done. Knowing we are there for each other and can rely on each other is the best gift ever. Knowing that I will get what I need at the time I need it. Knowing that the present really is a gift even when sometimes it feels like it isn't. Our gang is The Faithful Five and our faith is what makes each day OK. Our faith is what turns the lights on when it feels so dark. Your world may have not been dark, and that is just grand. But if it ever is, know that the darkness is just an illusion because light removes all darkness and where there is light there is love.

Until we meet again and hopefully soon,

Lots of love

Charlie xox

Oh wait, there is more. School started on Monday and.... There are plenty more adventures to share with you, good times and well, some challenging times, but that is life aye. There is always something worth sharing IMHO. I will be back so hopefully we can meet again soon!

ABOUT THE AUTHOR

Chris was born in New Zealand and travelled abroad for short holidays. Although working in IT in Auckland (of which 3 months spent working in Dallas) Chris has a creative side that she finally decided to capture on paper. Raised in childhood as a Christian she decided most of her troubles in adult life were from looking without instead from within. Chris has been stepping in and out of the spiritual path over the last few decades and in the last few years has now embraced her spiritual journey. She knows the spiritual path leads us into the direction of love, peace and forgiveness towards each other. Who could ask for a better world? ☺

www.ingramcontent.com/pod-product-compliance
Ingram Content Group UK Ltd.
Pitfield, Milton Keynes, MK11 3LW, UK
UKHW020421250726
13967UKWH00007B/2751

9 780473 595500